Three Little Kittens

For Jamie, Jacob, Nathaniel, and Mariska

The Library of Congress Cataloging-in-Publication data is on file.

ISBN: 978-0-89919-426-4 hardcover
ISBN: 978-0-89919-796-8 paperback
ISBN: 978-0-547-57575-9 paper over board

Manufactured in China
LEO 10 9 8 7 6 5 4 3 2 1
4500262983

Three Little Kittens

A FOLK TALE CLASSIC

Illustrated by
PAUL GALDONE

Houghton Mifflin Harcourt

Boston   New York

Little Kittens

they lost their
mittens,
and they began
to cry,

"Oh, Mother Dear, we sadly fear
Our mittens we have lost!"

Then you shall have no pie."

The
three little kittens

found their mittens
and they began to cry,

"Oh! Mother Dear, see here, see here.
Our mittens we have found."

"What!
found your mittens,
you good little kittens,

Then
you shall
have
some pie."
"Purr,
purr,
purr."

The three little kittens

put on their mittens
and soon ate up the pie.

"Oh! Mother Dear, we greatly fear
Our mittens we have soiled."

"What! soiled your mittens,
you naughty kittens!"

Then they
began to sigh,
"Meow,
meow,
meow!"

The three little kittens

washed their mittens,

and hung them up to dry.

"Oh! Mother Dear,
look here, look here,

Our mittens
we have
washed."

"What! washed your mittens,
you darling kittens!

But
hush!
I smell
a rat
close
by."

"Yes, we smell a rat close by.
Meow, meow, *meow!*"